To: John
From: Mommy
1985

Green Andrew Green

Green Andrew Green

by
ISABELLE HOLLAND

Illustrated by Pat Steiner

THE WESTMINSTER PRESS
Philadelphia

Book Design by Christine Schueler

First edition

Published by The Westminster Press®
Philadelphia, Pennsylvania

PRINTED IN THE UNITED STATES OF AMERICA
2 4 6 8 9 7 5 3 1

Library of Congress Cataloging in Publication Data

Holland, Isabelle.
  Green Andrew Green.

  SUMMARY: When Andrew Green actually turns green and suffers teasing and ostracization, he learns that power does not breed popularity: one must give love.
  I. Steiner, Pat, ill. II. Title.
PZ7.H7083Gr 1984   [Fic]   84-2402
ISBN 0-664-32714-1

Green Andrew Green

THE SUMMER I WAS TEN, I took a long walk to the End of the World. It wasn't as hard as I thought, but I had to do it when nobody was watching. My name is Andrew, and I started the journey during the weeks I was staying with Aunt Jessica and Uncle Robert at the shore.

The main reason I started is because I was looking for somebody to play with. Someone special and super. Somebody I didn't hate.

"Why don't you play with the other kids on the beach? At least two families have boys your age," Aunt Jessica said.

"They're different," I said.

"Different from what?"

"Different from me." I was watching my grammar

carefully. Sister Jones, where I went to school, was very careful about grammar.

"In what way?" Aunt Jessica asked. But I could tell from the way she asked it that she already knew the answer. She was just doing what grown-ups are always saying not to do while they are busy doing it themselves: pretending.

I looked at her. "May I be excused?" I said. I was not going to go along with her in all this make-believe.

"All right," Aunt Jessica said. "But remember not to go out into the sun."

"We can't keep the child in for the rest of his life," Uncle Robert said.

"Just how green do you want him to be?" my aunt asked him.

"I thought that word was never to be used in this house," Uncle Robert said.

Aunt Jessica looked cross. "All the positive thinking in the world is not going to make him less green."

"I like green," I said. "It's God's color."

"How do you know?" they both asked at once.

"Because he told me when he and I were talking."

"God talks to you?" I could see they thought I was making it up.

"Of course," I said, copying Miss Williams' manner at school: haughty, know it all. And left quickly. Because God and I did not talk. How can you talk to someone who lets you become green just because he forgot to make enough human color and ran out before he finished with you?

One day at school, Katie, a really horrible girl and my enemy, said, "What's the matter with you? Are you sick?"

"Of course not."

"Then why do you look green?"

"I don't look green."

"Yes, you do."

"No, I don't."

"Peggy," Katie said to another girl who was just as horrible as she was, "doesn't Andrew look green?"

Peggy stared. "Yes. I was noticing it before, only I thought it was because he was standing in the shadow. But we're in the sun now. He's green."

"And getting greener by the minute. Hey, kids. . . . "

It was a very bad ten minutes. Sister Hewitt came up.

"Andrew's green, Sister," Katie said.

"Nonsense, Katherine. And I've told you not to make personal remarks. There's the bell. Quick, everyone. It's time for class."

But later, when I passed her office, I heard her say on the phone, "But Andrew *is* a strange color, Mrs. Green. I thought they were just being naughty and wicked. But then in class . . . when I looked . . . "

I ran home.

"No more green vegetables," I said at first. I had never liked them.

The kids made up a rhyme:

"Green by name and green by face,
Andrew comes from a funny place."

After a while I stopped going to school.

"Don't you miss your friends?" Mother asked anxiously.

"I don't have any. Nobody likes me when I'm green."

Once the teacher had said to me, "More people say hello to you, Andrew, than to anybody else. That means you have a lot of influence."

"What's influence?" I asked my father that night.

"Well, I guess you could call it power."

I felt powerful. I could feel my chest getting bigger.

"Andrew's got a lot of clout," my father said the next morning in the car pool. I know, because Katie's father's in the pool too, and she told me.

"But you *don't* have power, Andrew Green," she said. "Especially not now when you're too green to be on a class team." The coach said my green would distract the others.

After I'd been home for a while, Father brought me a kitten.

"I don't like it," I said.

"Why don't you wait and see?" Mother asked.

"Cats are for girls."

"But you might get to like it," Father said.

"That's not the same as people liking me."

So the kitten went back to the shelter.

"You mustn't let what other people say bother you," Father said. But I noticed he stopped using the car pool to his office. Instead, Mother drove him to the station and he took the train. Then she'd come home and start me on a new diet.

I was perfectly healthy. Forty-eight doctors and two hospitals said so. But Mother kept thinking it was something I ate. The one thing that everybody saw was that indoors I was fairly green, but out in the sun I was very green indeed. So I stayed in and read my schoolbooks and hated the world and everybody in it, especially everyone at school. Even more I hated the color green. Most of all I hated myself.

Finally Father went to court and changed his name to Brown. But six weeks later I was even greener. That was when they sent me to Aunt Jessica and Uncle Robert at the shore.

It was true about my being greener out in the sun. So I remained in the living room with the television on most of the time. One day Uncle Robert went to play squash and Aunt Jessica made up her shopping list.

"I'm going to the shopping center, Andrew. Would you like to come? You don't have to get out of the car."

The previous week I had sat in the car while all the kids in the shopping center came and stared at me. They didn't all come at once. First one came, then he called another, and after a while there were about twenty. Finally one—a girl—opened the door.

"Are you sick or anything?"

"No," I said loudly.

"Well, then, why are you green?"

"Why are you pink?"

"I'm not pink," the girl said indignantly. "I'm tan."

Aunt Jessica and I didn't say anything on the way home. Finally, when we got there, she burst out, "There's nothing in your mother's family anywhere that would explain this." Aunt Jessica and Mother were sisters.

That had been the week before. Now she said, "You don't have to go shopping with me." And suddenly I knew she didn't want me to go.

"You're ashamed of me," I said. "Just like Mother and Dad."

"No, I'm not. How can you say such a silly thing?"

"Because it's true." It was funny. Until that moment it had never occurred to me, but now I knew it was true. And then I knew something else, and said, "But they're ashamed of me for different reasons. Dad's ashamed because he thinks if I just tried hard enough I could stop being green. Mother's ashamed because she thinks it's something she's done wrong."

"That's nonsense," Aunt Jessica said. "Your mother just needs a little rest." But I could tell she knew it was true.

"Well . . . " she said. She glanced at the television set, where a funny-looking man was flinging his arms around.

"Did you say your prayers this morning?"

"No."

"Well why not?" Aunt Jessica sounded alarmed. She's very big on church and God.

"Because I don't think it does any good. I've prayed and prayed not to be green any more and God hasn't done anything."

"Then it's not God's will to."

"Why not?"

"Stop asking why not!"

"Why?"

Aunt Jessica suddenly went bright red. Funny, I thought, Aunt Jessica goes red and it's nothing special. But I go green and everybody thinks I've done something awful.

"You think it's my fault," I said. "Don't you? Me being green."

"Well it's not God or your parents' fault, and there's no other explanation." She hesitated. "Not that we love you any the less."

"Who's we?"

"Stop asking so many questions."

"Why?"

Aunt Jessica picked up her handbag and stared at the man on the screen, who was still waving his arms and talking, but with no sound.

"You turned off the sound," she said severely. And then, almost accusingly, "Why?"

"No, I didn't," I replied.

"You must have."

"I didn't."

"I'll be back soon," she said and almost ran out the door.

When she'd gone I sat down and looked at the man on the screen. He was still flinging his arms around, and there was still no sound. Then suddenly, in a burst, I heard him say, "Some of us are from other planets." Then the sound and the man both disappeared. On the screen I saw trees and green and mountains and a river, but not just flat, as in a photograph. It was as though I were a part of them and walking through them. There was no sound at all, except a piping noise, like somebody playing a recorder the way that horrible Katie did in school in music class. Only this was nice. I walked closer to the set. Or perhaps, I thought, staring at it, the set was growing bigger.

The green field in front of me seemed to grow nearer and nearer. I could see every clump of grass. And everything was so green. . . . It was a green world where even the sky and the river and the tree trunks were just different shades of green, and it was beautiful beyond anything I'd ever seen.

I think I'll just take a walk there, I thought to myself.

The next thing I knew, I was beside the stream with the fields all around me. I looked down at my legs. They were exactly the color of the grass.

Suddenly, behind me, there was a bark. I turned quickly. There, down on his front paws, with his backside up and his tail wagging, was a green dog.

"You're green," I said. I'd never seen or even imagined a green dog.

He barked again. Then, finding a green stick, he came and put it at my feet.

Picking it up, I threw it as far as I could. It fell into the clear green river. The dog bounded in and swam to where the stick was floating downstream, got it in his teeth and swam back. Pausing beside the river, he shook himself. Clear green drops flew in every direction. Then he brought the stick back and put it in my hand and put his paw—a green paw—on my foot. Suddenly I noticed that my blue sneakers and blue jeans and white sweat shirt were the only non-green colors around, and they looked *hideous.*

Even the dog seemed to notice. He lifted his paw, looked at the sneaker, barked, and headed off.

"Underneath I'm just as green as you," I said.

But he barked again. Then he ran away.

"Come back, please come back!" I yelled. "It's only a color." But all I could see as he disappeared over the hill was his green tail.

I sat by the side of the river and stared at the green water. Supposing I went into it and never came out, I thought. Who'd care? Mother and Father preferred me human color to green. And besides, they only liked me when I had clout and influence and power to make people like me. The whole idea of going into the water seemed peaceful. I decided to go for a swim. So I undressed, put my clothes on the side of the river and dived in.

I went down, down, down, and then, when I thought my lungs would burst, I came up again. The air smelled and tasted and felt wonderful. I decided

I would postpone killing myself.

After a while I came out of the water. I rolled on the grass and then went to get my clothes. But they were gone. I went up the bank and then down and swam to the other side in case I had come out on the wrong bank. But the clothes weren't anywhere. I'll get cold, I thought. But I wasn't cold at all. The air felt just right.

I stood looking at the world and wondered what to do next. At least, I thought, there weren't any people around to make me feel strange or be ashamed of me. It was better to have no people than people who did that, wasn't it?

Yes, I told myself. It was. But I wished the dog would come back. At that moment I saw him. He came running back dragging something.

"Here," I yelled. "Come here!"

He tore over and put a bag at my feet. Inside, I could see, were my jeans, shirt, underwear, socks and sneakers. But they were now green. The jeans were kelly green, the shirt was light green. My underwear and socks were light green and my sneakers were a deep green.

"Somebody must have done this," I said.

The dog barked. When I had the clothes on he ran off—the same direction he'd come from. Then he stopped, barked, looked at me and barked again.

"All right, all right," I said. Plainly he wanted me to follow him.

We ran up a small hill. When I got to the top, there under a tree was a green girl. "Hi," she said.

I stopped. "Hi!" Everything about her was green, and yet she looked perfectly ordinary—like any other girl.

"You're welcome!" she said.

"Welcome about what?"

"I mean you're welcome that I fixed your clothes for you."

"I liked them the way they were," I said. "At least they weren't green the way everything else is."

I couldn't believe I was saying this. This was the first person in weeks who'd talked to me as though I were an ordinary human being, and here I was, picking a fight.

She stared at me. "I can always change them back," she said.

"How can you? You don't have any other color."

"Do you want them the way they were?" she said.

I didn't know what I wanted. So I just muttered something and looked away.

"Well?" she said.

"I don't see why I have to be something special to have people like me," I said aloud.

"Who said anything about not liking you?"

I stared at my feet. "Well, why did you make all my clothes green?"

"Because I thought they were meant to be green,

of course. Do you want them back the way they were?" she asked.

What I *wanted* was for her and me to be friends, but somehow color and my clothes had become mixed up in it.

"All *right,*" she said, and pointed both hands at me, all the fingers out.

"Pew, pew, spiddley dew.

Nobody stinks but you."

"I do *not* stink," I said.

"You do when you wear clothes that aren't the True Color. But that's the way you like them. Well, there you are! I hope you're happy."

I looked down. I now had on a blue shirt, orange jeans, and white sneakers with purple socks.

"That's not the color they were!" I said.

"Yes, it is! What are you talking about?"

"I didn't have orange jeans. Nobody has orange jeans."

"What difference does it make? There are only two colors, green and not-green. I have to go now, and so does Roderick."

"Who's Roderick?"

"My dog."

I looked down at Roderick, with his silky green coat, green floppy ears, and green tail.

"Hi, Roderick," I said, and put out my hand. Roderick wagged his tail but stayed where he was.

"He doesn't like not-green," she said.

Suddenly somebody was shaking me. "Wake up, Andrew! Wake up!"

I opened my eyes. There was the television set, off now, and there was Aunt Jessica.

"What on earth have you done to your clothes?"

I looked down. My jeans were orange and my socks were purple.

"It was the girl," I said, rubbing my eyes.

"What girl?"

"The green girl."

"Are you trying to be funny? There isn't any green girl. Just you. And that's enough." Then she patted me on the shoulder. "Not that we don't love you."

"No, you don't."

"Of course we do! How can you say such a thing?"

"Because it's true. You don't love me and Uncle Robert doesn't love me and Mother and Dad don't. And Roderick doesn't love me. You all stink."

And I got up and ran outside onto the beach. After that I didn't know what to do, so I walked slowly down to the water.

I was standing there when a black-and-white dog streaked past me, a stick in his mouth.

"Roderick," a girl yelled. "Come back." The dog stopped, turned around, put down the stick and waited, tail wagging.

I stared at him. Except for the fact that he was black and white instead of green, he was exactly like

Roderick . . . the green Roderick. I swung around. The girl walking toward me was the green girl, except that she wasn't green.

"Hi," I said.

She stopped, staring at me.

Suddenly, for a moment, I knew what she was thinking. It was exactly as though her mind was a tape playing in my head, which was acting like a recorder, the kind my father has. She was thinking, *Weird! A green boy with orange jeans and purple socks?*

"Are you from the circus?" she asked.

"No."

"Then why did you paint your face green?"

"Listen," I said, "you're thinking I'm a nut. I'm not—"

"Roderick!" she called out. "Let's go home." She turned and ran back the way she came. I watched her and Roderick disappear and then went back to the house.

"Go and change your jeans at once," Aunt Jessica said when I walked in. "Right now. Upstairs. And your shirt and socks. I've put your other clothes out on the bed. I'll take those to the thrift shop tomorrow."

Laid out on my bed were jeans-colored jeans and white socks, shirt and underwear, and on the floor were my other pair of sneakers.

"There's a girl on the beach," I said, bringing the

other clothes down when I'd changed. "She has a dog named Roderick."

Aunt Jessica stared at me. "There's no girl on our side of the beach. Not unless somebody new has moved in. And I don't know of any dogs. We're not supposed to have dogs here."

"Well, she's there," I said stubbornly.

"How old is she?" Aunt Jessica asked.

"About my age."

"As I said, there's no girl that age on this side of the beach."

"But I saw her!"

She stuffed the clothes I had given her in a shopping bag. "I don't know what's the matter with you, Andrew. At first I thought—your parents and I thought—you were just the victim of some unfortunate and dreadful disease. Now I'm beginning to wonder if it doesn't have something to do with your character, telling stories like that."

"I'm not telling stories."

But I knew she didn't believe me, and it was no use telling her about traveling into the television set, because that would just make it worse.

"You know God punishes those who break the laws."

"I haven't broken any laws. But it doesn't matter. God doesn't like me anyway. And I don't like God."

"That's a wicked thing to say."

"You'd say it too—if you were green."

"What I can't understand is how on earth you managed to find those colors *and* dye your clothes in the short time I left you to watch television. Just tell me how you did it, and maybe I can understand better."

I decided to tell the truth. "I took a walk through the television set into another world where everything was green. A girl, the same girl that I saw just now on the beach, except green, made my clothes green, and when I told her I wanted them back the old color she made them blue and orange and purple like you saw." I stopped talking, and we looked at each other for a moment.

"I want you to stay right here," Aunt Jessica said. "I won't be gone long. Now don't go out." She paused. "You may watch television if you like . . . although from what you said—oh, go ahead and watch it. I don't suppose it makes any difference no matter what you said."

When she'd gone I turned on the television set. The person I would like to have talked to was God, to tell him what I thought about the way I was being treated.

The teacher at Sunday school always said, "Now be good boys and girls or God will punish you."

Once I heard another teacher say to her, "That's an awful thing to tell them. It makes God sound so punitive."

"What's punitive?" I asked Mother later that afternoon. She was busy doing the crossword puzzle.

"Punishing." She glanced up at me, and I remembered that she had been angry with me that morning because I'd forgotten to clean my room. "As in when people don't clean their rooms they're not allowed to watch television for two days. . . . "

The next Sunday I asked the Sunday school teacher if God punished a person the way parents do.

"Of course," she said.

"But at least when your parents punish you, you know what you've done wrong. God never told me to do something or not to do something. So why should I be punished?"

"Is God punishing you?" she said.

"No," I replied. (I wasn't green then.)

"Well then, why are you complaining?"

"I just don't think God sounds very kind."

The teacher looked horrified. "That's a terrible thing to say. You'd better be careful. 'Be not deceived!' " she quoted in a loud, important voice. " 'God is not mocked: for whatsoever a man soweth, that shall he also reap!' " She sounded grim.

"God said that?" I asked.

"Yes."

"No, God didn't," the other teacher said. "Paul did."

"God was speaking through Paul."

"Well, how about, If your brother sins against you

28

seventy times seven you still should forgive him?"

"Who said that?" I asked. "I'd rather be on *his* team."

"Jesus the Fisherman," the second teacher said.

"You're just confusing the child," the first teacher said. I could hear them arguing as I walked down the hall.

Three days later I was green. Two months later I came here to the shore.

I watched Aunt Jessica get into her car. Then I turned on the television set. There was the man waving his arms but making no sound. I turned up the volume, but there was still no sound. Then I started changing stations, and the sound bellowed out.

Quickly I lowered the volume. I kept moving the dial and finally arrived back at the man waving his arms. Abruptly his voice came clear. "I told you some of us were from another planet, but you wouldn't believe me."

"Which one?" I asked.

"The trouble is," he said, "you don't understand about time."

"What's there to understand?"

"It's a box."

"What kind of box?"

"Like a TV box. The kind I'm speaking out of now."

"What are you talking about?" I asked.

He opened his mouth wide—and then he disappeared. I stared at the screen. The green countryside appeared and got larger and larger. I stepped into it, and there was Roderick—green all over, except that where his coat had shown black before, it was a darker green, and where it had shown white, it was a lighter green. He was standing in front of me, holding a stick in his mouth.

"I'm not going to pay any attention to you," I said. "It doesn't matter whether you're here or on the beach. You won't really play with me, you'll just pretend. So I'll pretend you don't exist." The green girl appeared behind Roderick.

"Pooh! You can't do that," she said. "You can *pretend* we don't exist, but you know and I know and Roderick knows that we do."

I held out my hand, one finger pointed, and said:

"Stink, spink, spew.

Nobody here like you!"

And she was gone.

I felt absolutely wonderful, important, huge. And very powerful.

Roderick put his stick down, trotted to the top of the little rise, looked over, went to the bank of the green river, then came back. He sat down and a little whimper came from him.

"Stop that!" I said. "I'm here. Let's play." I moved forward. He backed up. I put my hand out to pat him and he growled.

"All right!" I yelled. "You want to go where she is. Well, you can!" I pointed my finger.

"Stink, spink, spew.

Nobody here like you!"

And he was gone. I gave a shout. Just let all those people back at the shore and at school make fun of me again. They'd soon find out who had power!

"I have it!" I yelled, and the whole green world quivered and rippled as though it were a silk flag.

I went to the top of the hill and sat cross-legged under the green tree and had a wonderful dream in which I made everyone I didn't like disappear.

For a long time I sat there feeling immensely powerful. Then another feeling came over me, but before I could figure out what it was I went to sleep.

When I woke up I was lying on the couch in the living room. Aunt Jessica was sitting across from me talking to a much younger woman with a cat-shaped, pretty face, red hair and green eyes. They were both looking at me. "Hello," said the red-haired woman.

"Hi," I said and sat up.

"Have a good sleep?" Aunt Jessica asked. She seemed nervous.

"Yes," I said.

"Did you have an interesting dream?" the redhead asked.

"Are you a doctor?" I asked her. Somehow I felt she wasn't just an ordinary friend of Aunt Jessica's.

"Not exactly." She smiled. "Tell me what you dreamed."

"Dreams are secret," I said. "It isn't right to tell them."

"People tell me their dreams all the time. And sometimes I tell them what their dreams mean."

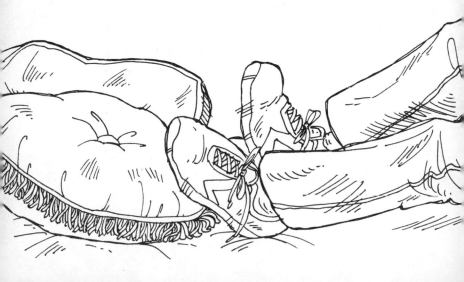

"I know what my dreams mean," I said. And suddenly I saw myself sitting under a tree having POWER, able to make anybody disappear. I pointed a finger at the redhead.

"Stink, spink, spew.

Nobody here like you!"

"Now what am I supposed to do?" Ms. Redhead said.

"I'm going for a walk," I said. I got up off the sofa. As I left the room the redhead said, "Hey, wait!"

Aunt Jessica called out, "Andrew, come back!" But I ignored them. I slammed the front door behind me and went out onto the beach.

Roderick gamboled up, his black black and his white white.

I picked up a stick and threw it.

He tore off after it. Then he ran back and put it at my feet. "Good boy," I said and threw it again.

We played like that for a long time. Then I raced him and he raced me. Then we played on the sand and rolled over and over.

Finally, after rolling over and over for the umpteenth time, I looked up and saw his owner.

"Oh, it's you," I said.

"Yes. It's me. And my dog. Come on, Roderick. Let's go home."

I said, knowing it wouldn't work:

"Stink, spink, spew,

Nobody here like you."

"That's a gross thing to say," she said. "If there were any more here like me we'd beat you up. Wouldn't we, Roderick?"

He gave a short, happy bark.

"Funny," she said. "When I came up you didn't look so green. Now you're greener than green. Maybe it has something to do with how mean you feel. Goodbye. And stink, spink, spew yourself."

I had to work very hard to remember that in the real world I had power and could make people disappear.

When I got back to the house, Ms. Redhead had gone.

"Who was the lady with red hair?" I asked Aunt Jessica.

"Just a friend," my aunt said.

"She asked me a lot of funny questions."

"You were very rude to her. I was embarrassed."

"All I do is embarrass people. If it's not because I'm green, it's something else. Who needs people? I want to go and live in the green country."

My aunt said in a kinder voice, "Because everyone there is green? So you won't feel embarrassed?"

"And I can make everyone disappear." I knew then I shouldn't have told her. She thought I was crazy before; she'd be sure I was now.

She stared at me for a long time. "If that's what you want, you can do that here. This part of the beach is very isolated. You don't have to talk to anyone. And you don't have to go shopping with me."

I wanted to say, But I don't have POWER here, but I was afraid she'd bring Ms. Redhead back and analyse me.

"All right," I said.

"You know your Uncle Robert and I are trying our best to make you happy here with us."

"I'm going out on the beach again," I said.

"You've become very difficult, Andrew. You used to be a nice little boy. Everybody liked you."

"I wasn't green then. When I got to be green that's all everybody could talk about—me being a freak. They don't like me any more. Now I don't like them." And I walked back out onto the beach, slamming the screen door.

Aunt Jessica called, "Andrew—wait!" But I went on walking.

I sat on the beach for hours. Nobody came. I thought about Katie and how horrible she was and about her friend and how awful she was. And my parents and uncle and aunt and the girl on the beach and Roderick and how awful they were, and how glad I was that they weren't there, and how wonderful it was to be absolutely alone. And then I started to cry.

When I stopped long enough to look up and take a breath, I saw, shimmering through all the tears I had been crying, a man, sitting on an upturned boat in front of me. The funny part was I couldn't remember the upturned boat being there before. And I had never seen the man. But he was sitting there, and beside him was a large dog, a German shepherd. He and the dog were staring out to sea. I waited for them to notice me so I could be rude to them.

Suddenly the dog barked and the man, still looking out to sea, said, "I don't know why we should notice you just so you can be rude to us."

It was eerie, and I felt my flesh give a little quiver. "How do you know I want to be rude to you?"

"Well, look for yourself!" And the man pointed. There, a few inches above the edge of the sea, was the TV-set time box, with a nineteen-inch screen. It was on a stand just where the tide was lapping in. And the water was whirling around the four legs of the stand, and flowing back and then in again. We were all there on the screen. My face was scowling, my eyes were red and I was shaking my fist at the man and the dog. The more I shook my fist the smaller they got.

"You see," I said. "I have POWER."

"I can see you have. It shows."

"It does, doesn't it? But I don't look like that!"

"Like what?"

"Glaring and ugly."

"How do you know you don't?"

"Because I've seen myself in the mirror."

"But have you looked at yourself in the mirror

when you're busy having POWER?"

I thought for a while. "No."

"Well, try it some time and see how you look."

"That's another thing. On the screen there I'm not green."

"I thought you didn't like being green."

"I don't. But that's not the point. If I'm green I'm green. If I'm not I'm not."

"Oh, I don't know. Some people get red and white, depending on how they feel. You get green or not-green."

I remembered how unfair God was being to me. "Yes, and it's not fair. Why should I be green when nobody else is?"

"But you weren't green on television."

I glanced across to where the television set was and found it wasn't there any more. "What happened to the television set?"

"It only goes on every now and then. The wiring around here is a little faulty."

"Well, make it come on again."

"Why?"

"Because I want to see myself on the screen again."

"But you didn't like the way you looked."

I remembered the way I looked and how awful it was. "I wish . . . " I said.

"What do you wish?"

A huge wish started growing inside me like a balloon, getting bigger and bigger.

"I wish . . . " I said.

"What do you wish?"

The wish was getting larger and larger. I glanced towards the edge of the water, and there was the television screen again with me in the middle. Huge.

"Why do I look so fat?"

"Because that wish you're wishing is getting bigger than you are."

I opened my mouth and said, "I wish I weren't green—permanently."

The wish inside me went *pop* like something exploding, and I was a normal size again.

"All right," the man said, getting up. "If that's

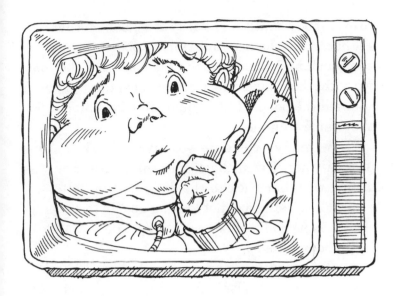

what you want—being ungreen—I'll see about it. Come along, Sirius."

"What kind of a name is that to give a dog? 'Serious.' That's crazy!"

The man smiled. And I found myself thinking of the sun.

"Who are you?" I asked. But he was gone. There was no boat, no dog, no television set, and I wasn't green any more.

It doesn't matter, I said to myself. I didn't like them anyway.

As I walked back to the house I counted up the people I didn't like. After I counted twice, they came to everybody: Katie and Peggy at school, Mother and Father, Aunt Jessica and Uncle Robert, the girl on the beach and Roderick, the redhead, and the man with the boat and the German shepherd. Then I counted the people I liked, and after I counted twice they came to none.

"How many people do you like?" I asked Aunt Jessica when I went back into the house. She was sitting with her back to the door, writing letters.

"Oh, lots," she said, not looking up. "In fact—practically everybody. How many people do you like?"

"Nobody," I said.

Aunt Jessica went on writing letters. "That's a shame," she said. "Isn't there any way you can get yourself to like them?"

The moment she said that I remembered I had POWER!

"Of course," I said. "I can POWER them to like me."

"You can do what?"

"POWER them to like me!"

"Don't shout! What was that word you said?"

"Power." I said it smaller, but it was still a big word.

"That's funny. I thought you said power."

"I did."

"Well," Aunt Jessica said, stuffing letters into envelopes, "if you think you can power people to like

you—although that's a funny way to use the word—
then you go ahead."

"You don't think I can?"

"I didn't say that."

"Well, I'll show you."

"You do that. And by the way, I thought you said
your problem was that you didn't like them. Not that
they didn't like you."

For a moment everything went upside down.
There was the ceiling at my feet and Aunt Jessica
writing at a desk that was the wrong way up. The
man and the German shepherd floated by in their
boat. The world was a crazy quilt of different greens.
Another moment, and everything went back
straight again.

"What are you going to do now?" Aunt Jessica
said.

"I'm going out to see if I can find somebody I like,"
I answered.

"That's a good idea." She spoke absentmindedly as
she poked around her stamp drawer. Just like a
grown-up, I thought as I left. All that fuss about me
being green, and then, when I became ungreen,
being too busy even to notice. And I was not going to
lower myself to point it out.

I walked out onto the beach and then along the
edge of the water. After a while I came to a piece of

driftwood and sat down. The moment I did, there was a loud squawk and then an angry *mee-ow,* and a large ginger cat crawled out from under the driftwood.

I didn't like cats to begin with. Only girls liked cats. So there was no point in using POWER to make this one like me. The cat stood there for a moment, pointing its nose up in little jabs as though it was trying to find a scent.

"Go away," I said. "I'm not going to waste any

power on you. You're not even a dog. You're only a cat."

The cat gave a long miaow and walked back and forth in front of me.

"Scat!"

The cat came and rubbed itself against my legs.

Then it started to purr. And the purr got louder and louder and louder.

"I told you to go away," I said, but I said it in such a low voice that even I couldn't hear it.

The cat jumped on my lap.

"You're hideous," I said, not touching it. One of its ears was torn. There was a sore on its shoulder with fur missing. And it looked dirty.

The cat settled itself on my legs, and a long, low rumble started coming out of it.

I didn't want to stroke the cat, but my hand went out as though it didn't belong to me and touched the ginger fur and then went down the length of the cat's back. The purring got louder.

"You like me," I said to the cat, still stroking. "That proves I can POWER you into liking me, even if I don't like you."

But the cat let out a low growl, sprang off my lap, and disappeared behind the driftwood.

"Come back!" I yelled. But there wasn't a sound, and there was no cat.

"I POWER you to come back!"

The whole world was empty.

I looked everywhere: under the driftwood, in the big reeds just behind, up above the beach, in the scrub and the woods. "Cat," I kept yelling, "I POWER you to come back!" But I couldn't find it.

After I had been searching for what felt like hours, I saw the girl and Roderick. "Have you seen a cat?"

I asked, as soon as I got near.

"What cat?"

"A big ginger cat. Ugly. With half an ear missing."

"No cats are allowed on this beach."

"Why not?"

"They're not tidy. If people have cats they're supposed to keep them inside. By the way, why aren't you green any more?"

"Because I POWERED myself not to be." Suddenly, in my head, the man and the dog and the boat floated by. "Sort of," I finished.

The girl looked at me, her head on one side. "I liked you better green."

"Well, it's too late for that," I shouted. "I ungreened myself."

"Why did you do that?"

"You ought to know. You made comments about my being green."

"So you were green. So what?"

"You thought it was pretty funny. You said so. I was tired of people thinking I was peculiar."

"And what's more, you keep talking about power. Why do you want power?"

"So I can make people like me . . . or do I mean so I can make me like people?"

"If you don't know, how should I know? Anyway, if you had all that power to ungreen yourself, then you can use it to make yourself green if that's what you want."

"Didn't you say you liked me better green?"

"Well, how do you like yourself, green or ungreen?"

"That's a stupid question. What does it matter what I think?"

"Who else is going to care if you don't? Besides, the whole subject of green is getting very boring. Instead of going on about it, why don't you use all that power you keep talking about to make yourself the color you want? Come on, Roderick, let's go!"

I closed my eyes and said in a loud voice, "I POWER myself to be green." Then I counted to five

and opened my eyes and very slowly looked down at my hands. They were purple.

"No — no — no — God!" I yelled. "I said *green!*"

I decided then to drown myself so everybody would be sorry and want me back. The tide was going out, but I figured that if I walked long enough I'd come to a place where I'd be drownable. But maybe, I thought, I'd take off my clothes. Aunt Jessica could send them to the thrift shop.

So I took off my clothes and was wading out into the water when I heard a loud, complaining miaow, and there was the ginger cat, walking back and forth on the shore.

It must have been in another fight somewhere, because the torn ear looked even worse and blood was coming down its face.

"Go back," I yelled. Even though I was only up to my knees, I could feel the pull of the tide and knew the cat would be carried out to sea.

But the idiot cat just yelled louder than ever.

"Get back, you stupid cat!"

Blood still streaming down its face, it started into the water.

There was nothing to do but come out. At that moment, from over the sand dunes, there rushed a huge black-and-tan dog followed by a terrible-looking man with a red face and a mean expression.

"Go get him, Thunder," the man yelled, but the dog was already after the cat.

"Stop," I screamed. "Stop! He'll kill him!"

"So what?"

I ran as fast as I could through the water, but the dog could run faster. I reached the cat just in time and held it over my head.

"I POWER you to stop!" I yelled at the dog.

Teeth flashing, the dog lunged.

"Help!" I cried. "Please—help!"

Suddenly from nowhere the great German shepherd leaped with a huge growl at the black-and-tan dog, which turned and ran away.

When I went into the house with the cat, Uncle Robert was there in the living room, reading his paper. As I came in, he lowered it.

"That's a really bad sunburn you have," he said. "Maybe you'd better see the doctor." He put up his paper and then lowered it again. "Funny, you used to be green. And what are you doing with that hideous cat?"

"He's not hideous!" I said.

Aunt Jessica came in. "So that's what's been bleeding all over my carpet. Put him out at once!"

"I will not!" But at that moment the cat took the matter out of my hands. With a great miaow he jumped out of my arms and ran towards the door that I had left open.

"Stop him!" I yelled.

"Certainly not!" Aunt Jessica said and opened the door wider.

"Cat!" I yelled and tore out.

But I couldn't see Cat anywhere. I looked all over the outside of the house and behind the shed where Aunt Jessica and Uncle Robert kept rafts and life belts and a surfboard. I looked in the garage and under the car. He wasn't in any of those places.

"Cat!" I yelled again. All I could think about was the blood coming down his gingery face, his muddy fur, his torn ear, the terror in his yellow eyes.

"Cat!" I cried and started walking up the beach. It was cold and gray. After a while I came to the piece of driftwood. It was quite large and had funny branches. I got down on my hands and knees and looked under the places where the branches met. By scrunching down and craning my head, I could see the whole inside the bottom part of the branch where Cat hid.

"Cat!" I yelled. "Please come out!"

There was no answering miaow or growl. I called again. I put my hand in and then my arm, first at one end of the branch and then the other. My arm wasn't long enough to reach the end, but I thought if Cat were there he would have bitten it.

"What are you looking for?"

I wiggled out from under the branch and looked up. The girl was there with Roderick.

"Cat. Have you seen him?"

"No, I haven't. And I wouldn't touch him if I had. He's dirty and mean."

I stared at her and could feel in me the beginning of a large red rage. "Who cares who you like?"

"I thought you didn't like anybody. So why are you sticking up for a yucky old cat? And anyway, green is an awful color and purple's worse."

I turned back and tried a few more times to talk Cat out of his log—if he was there. But there was no response.

"Your uncle and I have decided that maybe you'd be happier at home," Aunt Jessica said the next day.

"We seem to do things all wrong, and we feel we're not helping you. So your mother and father are coming to get you tomorrow."

I thought of Cat, bleeding in his hole. "No. I don't want to go."

"Why not? I didn't think you liked the beach. And you told me you didn't like anybody."

"Well, I was wrong. There is somebody."

"Who?" Both Uncle Robert and Aunt Jessica asked the question.

I decided not to tell them. You can never be sure what grown-ups will do with a piece of information like that. So I said, "It's a secret."

"I guess it's that pretty girl down the beach that's been coming over with her dog," Uncle Robert said, and winked at me.

I turned to Aunt Jessica. "I thought you told me there was no girl on the beach. That it all came out of the green country in the TV set, which meant my head."

"What green country? What TV set?" Uncle Robert said.

Aunt Jessica looked at him. "I hadn't told you that part yet." She frowned at me. "I had Dr. Rufus over to see Andrew—"

"I don't know any Dr. Rufus," Uncle Robert said, interrupting.

Aunt Jessica sighed. "Of course you do. She has

red hair and practices therapy in the city. She's here for vacation. I pointed her out to you on the beach the other day."

"You mean that smashing girl in the bikini."

"There are other aspects—"

"Can I be excused?" I asked.

"No." Aunt Jessica, who had been frowning at Uncle Robert, turned and frowned at me. "I want to talk about the person you like."

"Why?"

"Because I think it shows a marked improvement in you."

Maybe, I thought, she'll help me find Cat.

"It's Cat," I admitted, against my better judgment. "But I've lost him because you let him out. If you'd help me find him—"

"You mean to say that the person you like is that horrible flea-ridden animal you tried to bring in here? That mangy, dirty—"

I shot out of my chair. "I like him!" I said. "And I'm going to go and look for him again."

"Well, I called the pound and they're coming to break up the driftwood in case he's there. He's a stray—probably wild, maybe even rabid. We don't want him around here."

"But he's my friend!" How I knew that I wasn't sure.

"Your parents and Uncle Robert and I are doing

our best to find you a nice friend." Aunt Jessica paused. "Even a nice animal. We were thinking of getting you a pedigreed—"

I pointed my finger at Aunt Jessica.

"Spink, stink, spew!
Nobody here like you!"

But it must have been the wrong finger. She didn't disappear. Instead, she sighed. "Dr. Rufus said—"

"I'm sure she'd agree that Andrew should go home," Uncle Robert put in.

"I don't want to go home. I want to go to the End of the World." Where I got that from I didn't know. But I did know that it was a real place and that it was important for me to go there. In the meantime, I had to find Cat. I couldn't go there until I found him.

"I'm going out to find Cat," I said.

"I don't think you ought to go out now," they both said, and started closing in on me.

"You know it's because we love you," Aunt Jessica said.

"And it's for your own good," Uncle Robert chimed in.

"And your parents feel the same way," they both said.

"It's just because you don't like my color."

"Green was going far enough," Aunt Jessica said.

"Purple is going too far," Uncle Robert added.

"The girl—the one with Roderick—"

"Her name's Katie," Aunt Jessica said. "I just found out."

"But that's the name of the girl at school."

"What school?"

"She likes me green."

They both stopped. "That proves it," Aunt Jessica said.

"Proves what?"

"That you are not only a . . . a fibber, but you are probably seriously disturbed."

"I'm not seriously disturbed. I'm purple, I want to go back to green, and I have to find Cat."

"I want you to go up to your room and rest," Aunt Jessica said.

The next thing I knew I was in my room. Aunt Jessica and Uncle Robert had somehow backed me upstairs.

"Now just stay here. We'll be back soon," Aunt Jessica said.

"I know you'd much rather be at home," Uncle Robert added.

"It isn't that we don't love you," they both said.

After they left, closing the door, I heard the lock click.

Love, I thought, was a strange word. We love you, they said. And there they were on the other side of

the lock and here I was on this side.

"I love you," Father said, and decided not to use the car pool and changed our name to Brown.

"I love you," Mother said, and took me to another doctor and, when she said it again, decided to send me here.

"God is love," they said at Sunday school. They also said—or at least one teacher did—that God punished.

Love equals punish, I thought, like in algebra, like when you don't clean your room, which was why I was here and the locked door was there, in front of me.

Love obviously wasn't green or purple, because I had been both those colors and it didn't work. I wondered what color love was.

Or maybe it was a game, where you had to find the right color. If you didn't find it you lost, and people were allowed to hate you forever. Except, of course, that Katie began to like green after I stopped being green. It must be part of the game, I thought: Now you see it, now you don't. Love, that is.

Suddenly I wished I had a TV-set time box in my room, so I could turn it on and ask the man with the waving arms what colors love and hate were on other planets at the End of the World and what the rules of the game were there.

But there wasn't a television set. On the other

hand, the set was often where it wasn't supposed to be, like in the water, with the waves lapping around it.

I closed my eyes and tried very hard to imagine the television set across the room from the bed.

"Ink, stink, bumble, boom," I sang.

"TV set be in my room!"

And I pointed my hand to where I wanted it. Then I opened my eyes.

No television set.

"I POWER you to appear!" I said. I held out both arms.

Nothing. Absolutely nothing.

All I could see across the room were the chair, the carpet, the desk and, above the desk, a picture. Funny, I thought. I hadn't noticed the picture before. I got off the bed and went and looked at it. It showed a man, a boat, and a dog. Underneath were the words "The Fisher of Men."

Pooh! I thought. Whoever wrote that didn't know how to write. It was just the kind of thing I'd get an F for at school, writing *Fisher of Men* instead of *Fisherman.*

"Much good you are," I said to the picture. "Asking for a TV and getting you instead."

I walked back to the bed and sat down again. I made up a new spell for a TV set and turned to the corner of the room to try it out. But the spell never

got born. There was the TV set, its antennas waving around like ears.

But I hardly had time to notice that, because on the screen were some men in overalls, standing beside Cat's log, and near them a van with the word POUND on it.

"Maybe we should get a long pole and run it down the log," one of the men was saying.

"We might kill it, but that's okay. It'll save us time," the other one said.

"Or we could set the log on fire," the first one said.

Then I saw Cat. He was in my mind, but it was as though I had taken my mind out of my head and put it on top of the antenna like another TV screen. I walked over to my mind and looked at it, and then I saw it wasn't on top of the antenna but was on the screen. I could see the men outside the log. One of them had a box of matches in his hand. And I could see inside the log. Crouched far at the end was Cat. His eyes were round and yellow and burned in the dark with rage and fear. He opened his mouth and a terrible miaow came out. It was like me crying.

"I'm coming!" I yelled.

For a minute I thought I would make up a spell and use my POWER. At that, though, the television screen went dark and the TV set disappeared. There was nothing left but the picture of the Fisher of Men, the boat, and the dog.

"Mr. Fisherman," I yelled. "Help!"

Then I ran over to the window and saw immediately how stupid I had been to think I couldn't get out. Underneath was the porch roof and below that just sand, although I couldn't remember noticing them before.

In two minutes I was down on the ground and running. It was dark by the time I got to the log. But the van's headlights were lit and trained onto the only hole in the log where Cat could come out. In front of the hole crouched the black-and-tan dog that had tried to kill Cat before.

"We've got him now!" one of the men in overalls said. "You got the match, Willie?"

Willie nodded. "Yeah."

He was standing at the end of the log where I knew Cat was hiding. In one hand was a matchbox and in the other a match.

"Andrew!" Aunt Jessica said in a loud voice. "What are you doing out of your room? Go back at once!"

"Yes, and he's still purple."

I looked up. Standing near the van's headlights were Aunt Jessica, Uncle Robert, Dr. Rufus, Katie and Roderick.

The Enemy, I thought. I hate them. They hate me. Like in algebra, X equals green. Why weren't my parents there?

Cat! I mentally yelled. *I'm coming!*

I walked up to Willie, who was still holding the match.

"Light the match, Willie," the other man said. "What's that kid doing there?"

"He's supposed to be home in bed," Aunt Jessica said.

Enemy, I thought, I POWER you away!

>"Stink, spink spew,
>   Nobody here like you!"

But nobody moved.

Willie struck the match. It flared like an orange ball.

"Mr. Fisherman, Mr. Fisherman, HELP!" I cried. "I CAN'T DO THIS BY MYSELF."

Something hard and painful in my head cracked. Outside there was a huge wind and a flash of lightning. Then an enormous dog sprang. In the lightning flash I saw his body arch across the sky. He landed near the black-and-tan dog, who gave a loud yelp and ran away. Then hail came down, and I heard the clink of glass as the van lights went out. I could hear the people shrieking as they ran away.

"Now," said a voice near my shoulder. "Put your hand through the end of the log and get Cat."

"How can I put my hand through the end of the log? That's stupid!"

"Do you always have to argue? Do you or don't you want help?"

"Oh, all right!" I thrust my hand at the end of the log, knowing it would bounce and then he'd feel silly. Instead, I found my knuckles against wet fur.

"Cat!" I said.

He gave a squawk.

"I'm sorry! How was I to know the end was only wet bark?"

"Because you might have trusted me. That's how!" Mr. Fisherman's voice was still behind me. "Now why don't you bring Cat out?"

It took a long time. Cat was shaking and bit me a couple of times, but it was as though I was inside Cat and knew exactly what he felt like.

"It's okay," I said. "Bite away!"

Eventually I got him out, still clawing and biting. I held him against my chest for a while. He drummed his hind legs against my stomach and bit my ear. But I knew if he jumped down, the Enemy would get him.

"I'll just take care of his ear," Mr. Fisherman said. "Come here, Sirius, lick it for him."

I was pretty sure Cat would really bite then. But

he didn't. After the third lick the ear looked better and Cat started purring. Then a tear in his neck disappeared. Sirius's tongue looked black in the moonlight, and after a bit, instead of looking wet and matted and dark, Cat's fur looked silvery.

"He's going to like Sirius better than he does me," I said, grumbling.

"So what?" Mr. Fisherman said, feeding Cat a little fish on my shoulder. I could feel Cat's rough tongue licking the fish and the top of my arm at the same time. "Why does it always have to be either/ or? Green *or* human color. Purple *or* green. Human color *or* some other color?"

"Well, it isn't me that made the rule. When I got green, people hated me. The people at school thought I was funny. Dad stopped going in his car pool. He and Mother sent me to the beach with Aunt Jessica and Uncle Robert, and they locked me in my room and want to send me back home."

"Well, you aren't exactly rushing over with love yourself, are you?"

"But they hate me."

"I thought you hated them."

I had that strange upside-down feeling again. For a moment it looked as though Mr. Fisherman and the boat and Sirius were dancing on the sky, their heads hanging down.

"Queer, isn't it?" Mr. Fisherman said.

"What?" I had a terrible suspicion that he knew

what I was seeing. I was right.

"Sirius and me drifting by on our heads."

"It makes me feel funny. Like having a television set upside down." I paused. "Which reminds me. Do you think some of us are from other planets, like the man with the waving arms said?"

Mr. Fisherman looked at me. "Of course. But what difference does it make?"

"It makes a lot of difference. What are people on other planets like?"

"What other planets?"

I stared at him. "Other than the one we're on right now. Earth."

"We aren't on any planet right now. Haven't you noticed?"

There the planets were, all around us, great globes of gold and silver and fire and mist, going in their slow circles, some with little globes going around them.

"Where are we now?" I said.

"We're on the ninth cloud."

"What's that?"

"It's a sort of island. It's sometimes called the End of the World. A way station. You can go on, or you can go back."

"Go on to where?"

"Where do you want to go?"

I decided not to answer right away.

Mr. Fisherman was sitting in his boat, throwing

the fish in his boat over the side. They were swimming off like silver arrows.

"They're alive," I said.

"Of course. Didn't you expect them to be?"

"But they're swimming in the air like it was water."

"There's not that much difference."

"What would happen if Cat and I went out there?"

"Out where? Where would you be going to?" Mr. Fisherman stopped throwing the fish and looked at me.

"Home," I said finally. "Earth."

"Well, what would you want to have happen if you went home?"

"I'd like not to be purple."

"You're not purple. Didn't you notice?"

I looked down at my hand. Even though it was night, there was lots of light from the planets and the stars and the fish. Mr. Fisherman was right: My hand was not purple. It wasn't even green. It was human color.

"Terrific!" I cried. "Now people will like me."

"But I thought you told me that Katie preferred you green."

"Yes. And that probably means Roderick does, too. Can I be green for Katie and Roderick, and human color for everyone else?"

"Everyone in the world?"

"Well, everyone I meet."

"Supposing someone wants you brown?"

"Then I could be brown."

"You mean if you meet someone who wants you brown, you'll be brown, or if somebody prefers blue, you'll be blue."

"That's right!"

"In other words, you want to be a self-adjusting rainbow."

"What do you mean?"

"The rainbow has all colors—red, orange, yellow, green, blue, indigo and violet."

"What about brown?"

"It's there. All colors are in those colors, or a combination of them."

I thought about it for a while, stroking Cat. He was getting bigger and bigger and more beautiful by the minute.

"Maybe I could have one of those switches," I said finally. "When I found what a person liked I could switch on the right color."

"Is that what you really want? The PPS?"

"What's that?"

"The People Pleasing Switch. It's like the philosopher's stone. Everybody's been looking for it."

"It sounds super. That's exactly what I want!"

I could already imagine how wonderful it would be. For Katie I could be green. For Mom and Dad, human. For kids at school . . . I could just imagine walking down the school hall, flicking my switch, everybody following me, wanting whatever it was I had. I could feel myself growing bigger and bigger and more beautiful. Like Cat. "I'll take it!" I said, and then burst out: "It's like POWER. I can POWER people to like me."

"Is that what you want most?"

"Yes."

"What about *your* liking *them?*"

"That's not important."

"Why not?"

I stared at the Fisherman. It was funny, I thought. I was sure I'd grown bigger. But he was even larger in proportion to me than he had been before. In fact, I just about came to his knees and had to shout. "Because there's no POWER in liking people. Only if people like me."

"All right. We'll take you back to Earth."

"But this is a boat. You'd need a plane for that."

"Coming up."

And there we were, all of us—Mr. Fisherman, Sirius, Cat and me in a plane. We soared through the sky, whirled around the planets a couple of times and finally landed on Earth on the beach.

"Out you get. Here's your switch. It's attachable to your body and you can wear it anywhere."

I stared down at the metal cricket.

"See?" Mr. Fisherman said. He put it on my arm and it stayed. "Just think the color you want and press this." He started back to the plane.

"Cat!" I yelled.

"Cat's staying with us. Unfortunately, we haven't perfected a PPS for cats that works."

"What does that matter?"

"Suppose you met somebody who wouldn't like you unless you changed Cat's color too. What would you do then?"

"Nothing."

"But that might interfere with your great mission —being liked."

"But I'll have POWER!"

"You can't have both POWER and Cat."

"Why not?"

"Because you might—just might—decide to POWER Cat away if the last and only person in the world who didn't like you said they would if Cat weren't there. You'd have total, absolute approval from the whole world, except that you'd have to get rid of mangy, torn Cat."

"But Cat is beautiful!"

"Not here."

"I saw him, after Sirius licked him. He was wonderful!"

"What you saw was Eternal Cat, who can be seen as he really is only at the End of the World. Cat here on Earth is torn and mangy. Cat, come here!"

Cat jumped out of the plane onto the beach. I

couldn't believe what I saw: Cat slinking along the dark sand, ears torn, tail hanging. As he rubbed against my legs he had a terrible smell—like bad fish. I reached down and stroked him and he tried first to bite me. Then he purred.

"Can't Sirius lick him well and beautiful again?"

"No. You have things here that'll fix that. They're at a place called Vet's. But you'll have to find it."

"But they'll put Cat in the pound."

"No. Not if you tell them not to. Now you're going to have to choose quickly, because I'm due somewhere else. I'm not my own boss."

"Who do you work for?"

"We'll talk about that some other time."

"You mean I can have the switch *or* Cat?"

"That's right."

"I thought you didn't like either/or."

"There are exceptions. This is one of them."

"Well, it's not fair. Anyway, I didn't start this. I didn't make myself green in the first place." I had a sudden idea. "I bet your boss did that."

"Probably."

"Why?"

"Who knows? Maybe there was a lack of green in the universe and it had to be balanced out. Maybe you had to become ready to meet Cat. What would you have done about Cat before you were green? Anyway, what difference does it all make? Stop fussing and choose."

Suddenly there was the television-set time box in the waves again. On the screen I saw myself strolling down the school hall with everybody following. I saw Father getting into his car pool and saying, "You really ought to see Andrew's switch. Oh, and by the way, we've changed our name back to Green. . . . "
I saw Katie asking me to be her special friend. . . .
I saw Roderick preferring to play with me over anyone, even Katie. . . .

But I couldn't see Cat anywhere.

"Cat isn't there," I said.

"No," Mr. Fisherman said, "he isn't. Come on, Cat, let's go!" Mr. Fisherman walked across the sand towards the plane. Slinking behind him, stomach to the ground, was Cat.

I looked at the time-box screen, where I was still taking everyone's congratulations for something. Then I looked at Cat, who was getting ready to jump into the plane. Just before he jumped he turned and looked at me. There was no longer rage in his yellow eyes. Just pain.

Mr. Fisherman appeared in the door of the plane. "Come on, Cat. Jump in!"

Cat gathered himself.

"CAT!" I yelled. "Come back here! I CHOOSE YOU!" And I threw the magic PPS switch back into the plane.

Suddenly Cat was in my arms, torn, bloody, and smelling of fish. His purr shook us both like a small earthquake and drowned out the sound of the plane.

Then we sat on the beach and watched the plane soar up into the sky like a silver eagle and circle among the stars and planets before it disappeared.